Scat Bug, Run!

Written by: Kathy Ann Rogers

Illustrated by: Sarah Hance

Scat Bug, Run!

By Kathy Rogers

Illustrated by Sarah Hance

Publisher:

Granny's Press

PO Box 58305

Louisville, KY 40268-0305

502-526-7982

Library of Congress Control Number: 012951058

ISBN 9780985945701

This book is dedicated to Debbie Young. I wish you were here. Rest in peace.

I want to thank my support team, my husband Frank, sisters Cindy and Mary, friends Mag and Susan, illustrator Sarah and my Aunt Neta. I could not have done this without you.

10% of the proceeds of this book will be donated to the Mattingly Center.

1520 Baxter Avenue, Louisville, KY 40205

1130 Maple Brook Drive, Louisville, KY 40241

The Mattingly Center is a non profit, non denominational agency dedicated to providing day services to developmentally disabled adults. Many of these adults have multiple medical needs and do not fit the more traditional day services.

The Mattingly Center's two locations are in urgent need of repairs. Their funding is dependent on charitable contributions, grants, endowments, fund raising and the annual fund raising event.

Visit their website at:
www.mattinglycenter.com

It was wintertime in Montana and
Sarah could not play outside.

Her dad made a castle out of a
cardboard box and put it in the
basement.

Sarah would spend her days there
pretending she was a queen.

Suddenly, Sarah stopped playing in the basement.

"Why are you not playing in the basement?" her mom asked.

"It's dark and I saw a bug down there!" replied Sarah.

"The bugs are annoying and more afraid of you," her mother said. "All you have to do is turn on the light and say,

> 'Scat bug, run!

> I want to come down

> And have some fun.'

And all the bugs will run and hide."

Every time Sarah went to the
basement to play, she would turn
the light on and yell,

    "Scat bug, run!

    I want to come down

    And have some fun."

One day Sarah went to the
basement steps, turned on the light,
took a deep breath and yelled,

"Scat bug, run!

I want to come down

And have some fun."

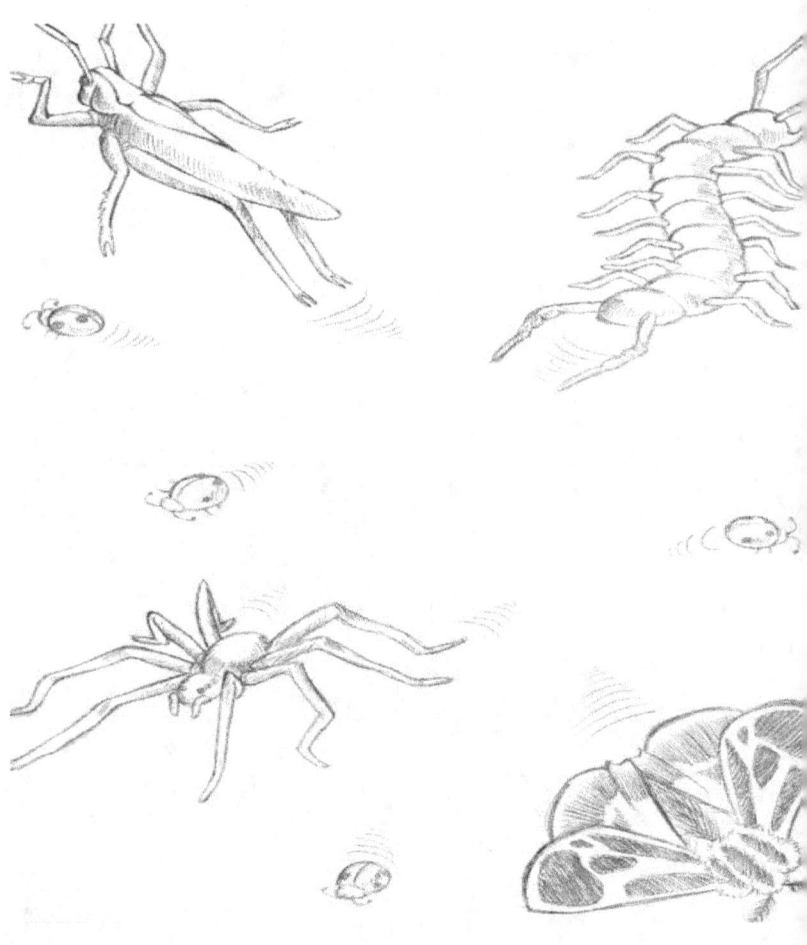

Sarah walked down the steps and in
the castle, sitting on her pillow, was
a centipede as long as her fingers
with more legs than she could
count. They both stopped and
stared at each other.

"What are you doing? Didn't you hear me tell you I was coming?" Sarah asked.

"Yes," the bug replied, "but I have some broken legs and can't run fast enough."

"What are you?" Sarah asked.

"I am a centipede, which are arthropods belonging to the class Chilopoda. I have one pair of legs per body segment. Some members of my family can be more than 12 inches long and have over 300 legs." The bug proudly added, "I am harmless, but you have to be careful because some bugs can hurt you."

Sarah asked, "Are you going to bite my leg off?"

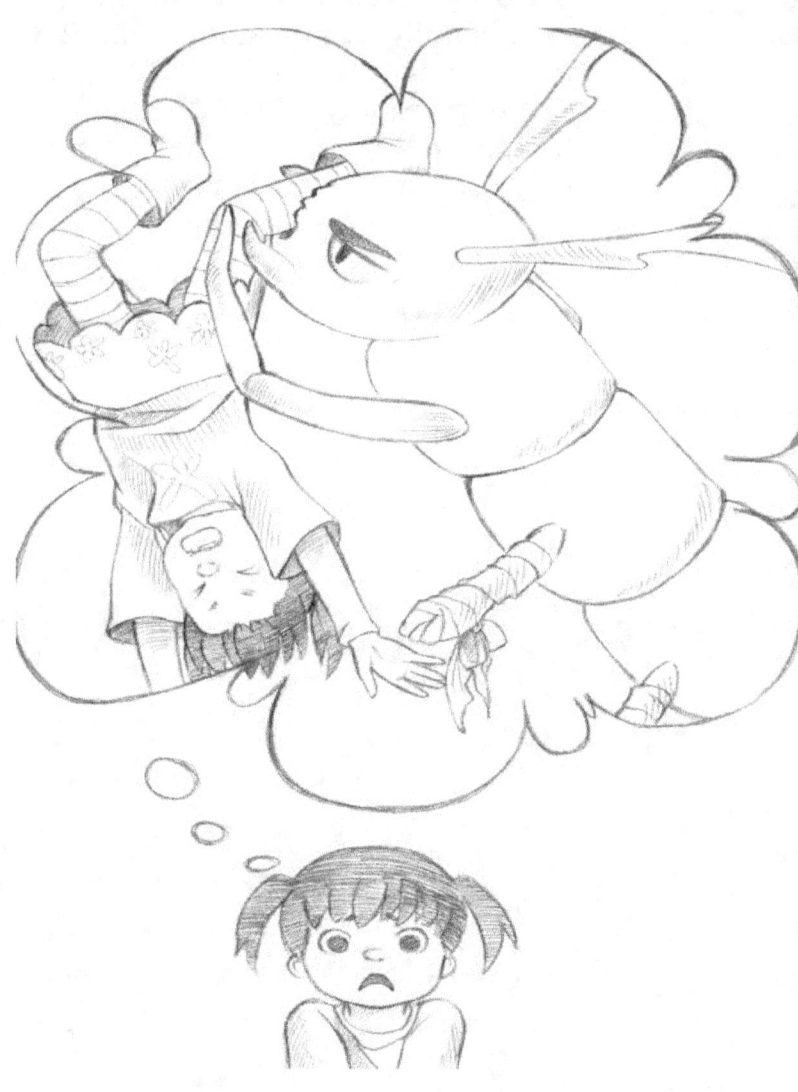

"No!" answered the bug. "My mouth is not that big, and I am so small I can't even reach your leg! Are you going to squish me like a pancake?"

"Why would I do that? I don't want to touch you," Sarah said. "Are you afraid of me?"

"Yes," the bug said. "I am afraid
that you would put me in a jar and
starve me."

Waving her arms, Sarah said, "That is silly, I was afraid you were going to crawl all over me."

"That is just as silly," the bug
replied.

They both stood there, too scared to move.

Finally, Sarah said, "I have an idea, would you like to be my king? I was going to have a tea party."

"Yes, I would like that," replied the bug.

Sarah set out some cookies and poured some juice. The bug was too small to eat anything, but the two became good friends.

After that, every time Sarah wanted
to play in the basement, she would
turn on the light and yell,

"Scat annoying bugs, run!

The queen and her king

Want to have some fun."

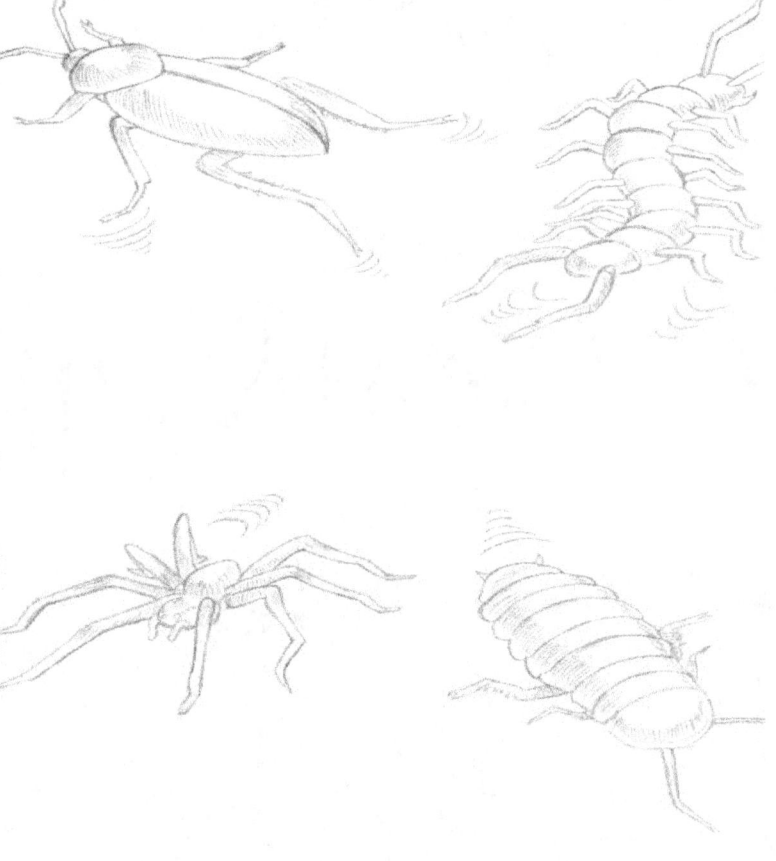

The mission of Granny's Press is to raise funds for organizations through the publications of books. These charities benefit education and improve the quality of life for the elderly and disabled adults.

To learn more about Granny's Press and the charities chosen, visit our website at:

grannyspress.org

Good night B and K. Grandma and Grandpa love you.

Author Kathy Ann Rogers is an "over 50" year old grandma of 2. She has previously been published in **Boys Quest Magazine**. This is her first children's book. Kathy is also a 15-year breast cancer survivor who refuses to let age stand in the way of achieving her goals. She lives in Louisville, Kentucky with her husband, Frank, and cat, Baby Sox.

Sarah Hance is a senior at the University of Louisville and will graduate with a Bachelor of Arts Degree in Fine Arts. This is Sarah's first book illustration and she has truly enjoyed the experience. After graduation, Sarah hopes to pursue an art career.

www.ingramcontent.com/pod-product-compliance
Lightning Source LLC
Chambersburg PA
CBHW071355130626
46556CB00005B/2191